The Snow Queen

Other brilliant stories to collect:

Aesop's Fables
Malorie Blackman

Hansel and Gretel
Henrietta Branford

The Goose Girl
Gillian Cross

The Twelve Dancing
Princesses
Anne Fine

Grey Wolf, Prince Jack
and the Firebird
Alan Garner

The Three Heads in
the Well
Susan Gates

The Six Swan Brothers
Adèle Geras

The Seal Hunter
Tony Mitton

Cockadoodle-doo,
Mr Sultana!
Michael Morpurgo

Mossycoat
Philip Pullman

Rapunzel
Jacqueline Wilson

Rumpelstiltskin
Kit Wright

The Snow Queen

Retold by
Berlie Doherty
from the original story by
Hans Christian Andersen

Illustrated by
Siân Bailey

SCHOLASTIC
Home of the Story

To the Children of Edale School

Scholastic Children's Books,
Commonwealth House, 1–19 New Oxford Street,
London WC1A 1NU, UK
a division of Scholastic Ltd
London ~ New York ~ Toronto ~ Sydney ~ Auckland
Mexico City ~ New Delhi ~ Hong Kong

First published by Scholastic Ltd, 1998

Text copyright © Berlie Doherty, 1998
Illustrations copyright © Siân Bailey, 1998

ISBN 0 590 54385 7

Printed by Cox and Wyman Ltd, Reading, Berks.

8 10 9

The right of Berlie Doherty and Siân Bailey to be identified as the
author and illustrator respectively of this work has been asserted by
them in accordance with the Copyright, Designs and
Patents Act, 1988.

Long ago in the cold north there were some wicked imps. Just for something to do they made a mirror. It wasn't like any other mirror. It made roses look like cabbages and birds like flying toads. It took the beauty out of everything, and if the object had an ugly heart, the mirror found it and

reflected it. The imps had great fun with that mirror.

They dared each other to show it to the most beautiful creature on the earth, the Snow Queen. "Go on, you do it," they cackled to each other. "Let's see how deep her famous beauty really is."

Well, the Snow Queen loved mirrors. She tossed back her long white hair and smiled, but all she saw in her reflection was her black and evil heart.

"How dare you show me this!" she screamed.

She was so angry that she struck her fist into the mirror and broke it into a thousand pieces, which shattered into the night sky and looked, for a moment, like stars. But then the sparkles of dust floated through the air and some of them landed in people's hearts just as if they were splinters of glass, and turned them to ice. The wicked imps screeched with laughter.

"Look, look what our mirror's done! There'll be some precious mischief now! It's better than ever!" And they scurried into their slimy holes

and waited to see what would happen next.

Well, it happened to a boy and girl called Kay and Gerda. They lived in the top rooms of very tall houses that faced each other, in the town of Amsterdam. They didn't have gardens, but they each had window-boxes where they grew their flowers. There was a bridge from Kay's window

to Gerda's, so they could walk across
to each other's rooms high above the
streets. And on the bridge there grew
a rose tree that belonged to them
both. In summer they used to watch
the flowers opening out.

"We count the petals on our tree
A rose for you, a rose for me."

That was their song.

And in the winter, when it was too
cold to play out and the frost made
feathery patterns on the windows,
Gerda would warm a coin and hold it

against the glass to melt the ice. Then she would look through the spyhole and see Kay looking at her from his window. He would run down his stairs and climb up to Gerda's room, and together they would listen to the tales her grandmother told, all about the animals she used to talk to. The snow would be flurrying against the window like a flock of white butterflies, and one day Grandmother told them to watch out for the Snow Queen, who had a wicked heart.

"If she ever came in here I'd put her on the stove and melt her!" Kay said.

That night in bed, Kay saw the Snow Queen. He opened his eyes and there she was, all in a shimmer of silvery light, peering at him through his frosty window and laughing down at him — but when he reached out to the glass she disappeared, as if the touch of his warm hand had melted her away. Or maybe he had only dreamed he saw her. That could be it.

But he should not have forgotten about her. Summer came again. Grandmother brought them both presents from the market — a pair of red shoes for Gerda, and a pair of boots for Kay. They wore them at once, even though Kay's were a bit big for him and creaked when he walked. "I like them like this," he said.

"You sound like a squeaky mouse!" laughed Gerda. "And aren't my shoes beautiful! They're my treasure!"

They walked backwards and forwards across their flower bridge, and suddenly a wild wind whipped around them, glittering with silver dust. They clung to each other. Some of the dust went in Kay's eye and drifted down to his heart. It stabbed him there as if it were a blade of ice, and he

gasped out loud with the pain. He thought he was going to die.

"Kay! What's the matter?" Gerda asked, but he pushed her away roughly.

"Leave me alone. I hate you," he said.

She stared at him, not understanding what had come over him.

"Go away!" he shouted.

Gerda didn't know that he had splinters of glass in his heart, and that it had already turned to ice. How could she know? "Can't I help you?"

"Go away. I can't bear to look at you," he said. "You're so ugly."

He tore down the rose tree that they loved so much. "Pooh, it stinks!" he said, and threw it over the bridge into the street below, where the carriages trundled across it and mashed it into the ground. And then he ran into his house, shouting to her that he never wanted to play her silly games again. "And I hate these stupid squeaky boots!"

"I don't know what's happened to Kay," Gerda sobbed, and the grandmother put her arms round her and comforted her. She thought in her heart that she knew what had happened,

but she said nothing. What could be done?

Before long, summer turned to winter and petals of snow came drifting down from the sky. Gerda pressed a hot penny to her window and made a hole in the ice. Imagine how happy she was to see Kay looking at her from his window across the bridge.

"Kay! Will you come and play

now?" she laughed, but he shouted back, "Don't be stupid. I'm looking at the snow crystals. Anyway, I'm going to play out with the big boys."

He stomped down all the noisy stairs of his house with his old sledge across his shoulder, and went to the far field at the end of town where all the older boys were playing. They laughed when they saw him, because everyone knew how sour and grumpy he was; not much fun in him at all. They were pulling each other about on their sledges, but nobody wanted to pull Kay along.

Then into all the clamour and laughter there came the sound of galloping hooves, and the whoosh of a sleigh that was rushing across the ice. A team of white horses with flickering manes was pulling a sleigh that glittered like diamonds. Driving it was a woman dressed all in white, looking neither to the right of her nor to the left of her. She reined in the horses and came to a stop, and everybody could see how beautiful she was.

"How about hitching a ride on that!" said one of the boys, and the others all whistled and shook their

heads. Nobody dared, it was so grand. Besides, it was so fast.

But Kay ran across to it. "I will!" he shouted. "Just watch me."

Well, the boys didn't believe for a second that he'd do it, but he did. He tied his sledge to the back of the silver sleigh. As soon as he clambered back on to it again the beautiful woman laughed, and Kay knew at once that he had heard that laugh before. The woman cracked her whip and away sped the horses, and the sleigh behind it, and behind that came Kay, bumping along on his old wooden sledge —

and behind him, all the boys of Amsterdam, until they stopped, gasping for breath.

Kay clung on to his rope for dear life. "Stop! Stop!" he shouted, as he was flung from side to side of his sledge. "Please stop!" Bit by bit his battered sledge dropped to pieces, so he was being dragged on his stomach along the ice. "Stop!" he screamed, and, at last, she did.

"Climb up into my sleigh, child." She wrapped a warm fur cloak round him. "Now, Kay. Don't you know me?"

And he did know her, of course. "You're the Snow Queen, aren't you?"

She put her arm round him and kissed him. "You're safe with me," she said.

She pulled at the reins and once again the sleigh started forward, but this time it rose up into the night sky, among the stars and the moon. Sometimes Kay slept and sometimes he was awake, with the wind cold on his face. They flew across land and they flew across sea, they flew across white mountains to the far, far north of the world where nothing moved.

Everything they could see was frozen into solid ice. The Snow Queen whipped her horses again and down and down they galloped, until they came to a palace that was made of blue ice.

Deep inside the palace was a great hall that glittered and rang with the tinkle of icicles. The Snow Queen said, "This is my home, and it is your home, Kay. For ever."

Kay loved her so much that all he wanted to do was to stay with her. He forgot about his home and his family. He forgot all about Gerda.

People said that Kay would never come home again. They watched out for him until the end of winter, and then they gave up watching. They said that he was dead. When Gerda heard them saying this she knew she must try to find him. She kissed her sleeping grandmother goodbye and ran out of the house, down to the river and along its banks until she was out

of sight of the town. She was sure that the river had swallowed him up, and that the river could bring him back. She took off her new shoes and threw them into the water, saying, "River, I'll give you my new red shoes if you'll only tell me where Kay is." Whether the river knew or not it wouldn't say, but would only laugh.

Gerda knew she must carry on searching. She slept in a garden of flowers and when she woke up and saw the roses she thought of Kay and knew she must carry on searching. She heard the birds over her head

singing, and asked them if they knew where Kay was, but whether they did or not, they wouldn't say.

So Gerda walked on into the cold of a forest, and there she met with a crow who asked her where she thought she was going in her bare feet.

"I'm looking for my best friend, Kay," she told him. "People say he's dead but I know he can't be. Can you help me to find him?"

The kind-hearted crow wanted so much to help her that he flew to a castle to ask his sweetheart, and she sent

him back with a message to say yes, a boy just like Kay had turned up that very day and married the princess.

"Life's full of little surprises, isn't it!" the pleased crow said.

Gerda ran through the forest and tiptoed through the castle to the very room where the new prince lay sleeping. She saw his golden hair and "Kay!" she called to him, but when the boy sat up she saw that it wasn't Kay at all. And there was the princess, demanding to know what Gerda was doing in her castle with no shoes on her feet.

"I'm looking for my best friend, Kay," Gerda told her. "People say he's dead but I know he can't be."

"Poor you," said the princess. "But you can't go on like this."

She gave Gerda warm clothes to wear, and strong boots to put on her feet, and a golden carriage lined with biscuits and peppermints to ride in. She kissed her goodbye and she and the young prince with the golden hair, the crow and his sweetheart all wished her luck in her search for Kay.

Deep in the blue heart of the palace Kay spent his days moving blocks of ice across the frozen floor, just to entertain the Snow Queen.

"Can I go out?" he asked her, weary of his task. He wanted to ride away with her when she went on her journeys.

"Where to? What for?" she laughed, and her laughter was like the shattering of glass. She stroked his hair. "One

day you shall have the freedom of the world!"

"Will I have a new sledge?"

"Yes, that too!" she called, as she rose away from the palace in her gleaming sleigh. "But first you must find me the secret of the universe, or you will never be free."

And so Kay toiled on, trying to make patterns with his ice blocks to solve the great mystery. And he was all alone in the great hall, and had forgotten how to laugh or how to sing.

Gerda hadn't travelled more than a night and a day when her coach was raided by a band of robbers. They killed the coachman and would have killed Gerda too, if the Robber Queen's daughter hadn't said she wanted her for a playmate. She stole her boots and muff and then bundled Gerda into the hall of the robbers, which was flickering with candlelight and reeking with the smells of robbers

and animals. The bearded Robber Queen sang lustily and did cartwheels along the great long table, putting her great fists in all the plates of food, but the Robber Girl wouldn't let Gerda stay and watch. She pulled her into her room to look at her pigeons and her pet reindeer.

"His name's Baa-baa," said the Robber Girl. "Go on, give him a kiss!"

But to her great surprise Gerda cried because the animals weren't free. "You're an odd one!" the Robber Girl said. "But you'll have to be my friend or Ma will have you for supper."

"Would she really?"

"Snip snip snee! I'll say she would! Couldn't you see her sparking her greedy little eyes at you?"

The Robber Girl slept with a dagger under her straw mattress in case Gerda tried to escape. But during the night something amazing happened. Gerda heard the pigeons talking together.

"We know where Kay is!" they cooed. "We do! We do! He's with the Snow Queen."

"The Snow Queen!" said Gerda, remembering Grandmother's stories.

"But where does she live?"

And the reindeer sighed and said, "Ah! The Snow Queen! She lives in Lapland, where I come from. If only I were free to wander in the snowy mountains again!"

Gerda woke the Robber Girl and begged her to let the reindeer take her to Lapland.

"Reindeers can't talk," said the Robber Girl crossly. "And besides, he's my pet. And anyway, I want you to stay here to be my friend."

"Then you'll know how I feel," Gerda said. "I want to find my friend,

Kay. People say he's dead but I know he can't be. Please help me."

The Robber Girl stared at Gerda, and knew she would have to let her go. She helped her to sneak out of the robber hall and put her on Baa-baa's back. "Goodbye, sloppy chops," she said to him. "Look after my friend."

They galloped through dark forests and climbed up into the white-headed

mountains, and around them wolves howled and ravens croaked. At last they came to Lapland, and by this time Gerda was almost frozen stiff with cold. Baa-baa hammered with his antlers on the door of a tiny house until an old woman opened it up. She had eyes as flat as fishes and layers of clothing like birch bark hanging on her skin.

"Oh, it's you is it?" she said. "What do you want?"

Gerda was so cold that she could hardly speak. "I'm looking for my friend. The Snow Queen has taken him."

"Well, she's gone to Finmark," the old woman said. "Now don't bother me with your tears. You'd better come in and warm yourselves with a bowl of fish stew."

While Gerda and Baa-baa were eating, the Lap woman wrote a message on a piece of dried fish and told them to take it to her friend the Finn woman. So Gerda climbed on to the reindeer again and on they went. Baa-baa's hooves chimed on the frozen earth. Nothing moved around them; no streams, no birds. The whole world was standing still. And they came to

Finmark.

"How can anything live here?"
Gerda asked. They found a house that
was buried so deep in the snow that
all they could see was blue smoke
coming from a hole. Gerda had to
climb down through the chimney, and
the reindeer followed her, protesting
loudly that he'd rather stay outside
and freeze than go indoors and sweat
to death.

"Get me out of here!" he bellowed.
"I'm going to faint."

There inside the smoky darkness
of her den was the oldest woman

Gerda had ever seen, with hardly a stitch of clothing on because it was so hot inside her house of snow. It was almost as if she was expecting Gerda. She held out her hand for the piece of fish and read the message, nodding and muttering. Then she put the fish into a stew that was bubbling on the fire, and sank into such a deep silence that Gerda thought she had fallen asleep and forgotten about her.

"Please will you help me?" she whispered, trying not to cry.

"Yes, wake up and help her," said the reindeer, scratching the old woman with his antlers. "Her best friend Kay has disappeared, and everyone says he's dead, but she knows he isn't."

"I know all that," said the old woman. "Don't hurry me." And she closed her eyes again.

"You know everything," the reindeer went on, "but all you can do is sleep. Can't you tell Gerda what she must do?"

The old woman didn't even bother to open her eyes. "No one can help her." She mumbled as if she was in a dream, although in fact she was think-

ing so deeply that she had travelled round the world and back in her head. "She's managed to come all this way in her bare feet, all for the love of a friend. What more could anybody do?" And then she dropped her voice still lower, so Gerda couldn't hear her over the crackling of the fire, and the reindeer only caught the words because his ears were so big. "She has such goodness. She has it in her heart to find Kay, and she will."

Then she opened her eyes and stared at Gerda. "Are you brave enough to go into the Snow Queen's palace on your own?"

"Yes," said Gerda, though she couldn't help trembling.

"It's only ten miles from here. Have some fish, and off you go."

The reindeer left Gerda in the garden of the Ice Palace, and said goodbye sadly. He was afraid for her, but he knew she had to go in alone. Gerda put her arms round his neck. She thought she would never see him again.

She was alone, and there in front of her with its lofty blue towers was the palace of ice. The guards rushed up to

kill her but she walked steadily towards them.

"Why should we let you in?" they shrieked around her.

"Because Kay is in there, and I love him."

And they fell away from her like snowflakes.

Deep inside the palace, in the very heart of it, Kay sat and stared at his

blocks of ice. The Snow Queen laughed at his efforts to solve her mystery.

"Are you satisfied with that? Try again, boy!"

He no longer had the strength to push the blocks around, but stared at them until his brain was as numb and cold as his body. His heart was like a fallen bird inside him, hardly fluttering.

And it was there that Gerda found him. He was blue with cold and his eyes were like glass, staring, just staring. "Kay!" she shouted. She ran to

him but he took no notice of her, as if he couldn't hear her or see her.

"Kay, Kay, it's me! Look at me. I can't tell if you're breathing."

And still he took no notice of her, but stared at the blocks of ice.

"Kay, please speak to me! I've come all this way to find you. They all thought you were dead, but I knew you weren't. I gave away my red shoes so I could find you. Don't you remember me at all?"

She put her arms round him. "We count the roses on our tree. A rose for you, a rose for me," she whispered.

He turned his head slowly to look at her.

She tried again. "We count the roses on our tree..."

"A rose for you, a rose for me!" he whispered, and at that moment he knew her. He started to cry, and the tears warmed his eyes and he could see her. His tears ran down into his heart and melted the ice around it.

Gerda pulled him to his feet and started to dance round with him to warm him up, and as they danced the blocks of ice began to move too, all on their own. They skated together to

form a pattern of letters.

"Eternity. They're spelling Eternity!" Kay shouted. "That's the mystery! I'm free, Gerda. I'm free!"

When the Snow Queen saw Gerda and Kay running hand in hand out of her palace what could she do but toss her head and laugh. They were nothing to her now. She was bored with her game. What did she understand about

the power of love? What did the wicked imps know about friendship? Nothing.

Baa-baa was waiting for Gerda and Kay in the garden. He took them back to the Finn woman, and she gave them food for the rest of the journey. They met the Robber Girl in the forest, and they walked on until they came to where the spring flowers were growing. They walked on to where the rivers were running free, and all the city bells were ringing. They were home.

They ran into the house and up

the stairs, and there was the grandmother waiting for them with her
hands in her lap as if they had never
been away. They went to sit on the
flower bridge, and laughed to find
that their chairs were far too small for
them now.

And it was summer again, in that
place of long ago.